# Hooray! Hooray!
# I sit! I stay!

HODDER CHILDREN'S BOOKS

First published in Great Britain in 2016 by Hodder and Stoughton
This paperback edition published in 2017

Text copyright © Mick Inkpen 2016
Illustrations copyright © Chloë Inkpen 2016

Hodder Children's Books
An imprint of Hachette Children's Group
Part of Hodder and Stoughton
Carmelite House
50 Victoria Embankment
London EC4Y 0DZ

A CIP catalogue record for this book is available from the British Library.

ISBN 978 1 444 92953 9

Printed in China

An Hachette UK Company
www.hachette.co.uk

# Fred

## Mick & Chloë Inkpen

Hodder
Children's
Books

I am not best in class.
But I'm not last!
I passed my test
along with all the rest.
At last I stay away
from cars and poo!
I know just what to do.
When called to come
**I do not run away!**

(Not often anyway.)

And I can fetch a stick.
Or ball.
I come when called.
And that's not all. . .

I sit! I stay!

I do not
run away.

# Hooray!

'Fetch!'
    and 'Sit!'
and 'Stay!'.
    I understand them all.
Those are the words I know.

And 'Ball!'
    and 'Walk!'
and 'Park!'
    and 'Bed!'.
I know those too.

But what is. . .

. . .'Fred'?

'Fred! Fred! Fred!' they say.
They say it all the time.
'Fred! Fred! Fred!' all day.
(You whisper it sometimes.)

If only I could Fred.
But Fred? It makes no sense.
They laugh and shake their heads.
They say I'm dense.

But I will Fred one day.
I know I will.
If I can Fetch and Sit and Stay,
I'll Fred. I know I will.
And they will clap and say,
'Good Boy!'

# I know they will.

There is another dog upstairs
where I am not allowed to go.
I saw him once.
I wonder if he knows
what Fred is all about
and why they shout it
all the time.

# He looks like me!
He has my ball.
He has no smell at all.

I'm chasing pigeons in the park
which I am not allowed to do.
I like the way they flap about.
I think they like it too.

And if there ar

No pigeons, a duck will have to do!

There is that other
dog again!
The dog I saw
the other day!
And look!
He has my ball again!
I wonder if he wants to

play!

Paddle!
Struggle!
Bubble!
Trouble!
Kick!
And splutter!
Choke!
And sink. . .

# 'Fred!'

I hear.
But cannot
think.

A scream!

A dash!

A jump!

A splash!

A foot!

A face. . .

. . .it's you!

# I'm safe!

I shake the water
from my ears.
I lick your face.
I taste your tears.

'Oh Fred,' you whisper,
'Fred. Fred. Fred.'

A **light** goes on
inside my head!

I stare into your eyes
and blink.
I think a thought,
a thought that thinks...

Fred is a **name!**

Fred is my name!

And suddenly I see
that I am Fred!
That Fred...

...is **me!**

I have been Fredding
all the time!
Fred is a name.

And it is **mine!**

I whizz around.
I make you laugh.
I look at you.
You say I'm daft.

I sit for you.
I lift my paw,
   then jump into
   your arms once more.

I nudge your nose.
Your cheek is soft.
I try to wag
   my tail
**right off!**

There's nothing left
for me to do,
 except to run
back home
  with you.

I am very fond of you.
You smell pondy too.

I drag my blanket
from my bed,
and snuggle up
with you instead.

I think
the thought
inside my head,
the thought
that **knows**
that I am . . .

. . . Fred.